Out in the shower, honeybees buzz by,

Soon others come inside,
out of the rain.

flying between raindrops to stay dry.

Suddenly the shower ends,

and the last few raindrops splatter down.

All together, the rabbits hop
out onto the lawn . . .

. . . to taste the wet grass,
and play rabbit tag
in the sun.